THIS WALKER BOOK BELONGS TO:

____

____

____

Charles Dickens

First published 1843
This abridged edition first published 1992
by Walker Books Ltd, 87 Vauxhall Walk, London SE11 5HJ

This edition published 2003

2 4 6 8 10 9 7 5 3

This book has been typeset in Cochin

Printed in China

British Library Cataloguing in Publication Data:
a catalogue record for this book is available from the British Library

ISBN 0-7445-9846-X

www.walkerbooks.co.uk

CHARLES DICKENS

A CHRISTMAS CAROL

abridged by VIVIAN FRENCH

illustrated by PATRICK BENSON

WALKER BOOKS
AND SUBSIDIARIES
LONDON • BOSTON • SYDNEY • AUCKLAND

MARLEY WAS DEAD. *Scrooge knew he was dead? Of course he did. Scrooge and he were partners for I don't know how many years, and Scrooge was Marley's sole friend and his sole mourner. And even Scrooge was not so dreadfully cut up by the sad event, but remained an excellent man of business on the very day of the funeral. Oh! But Scrooge was a squeezing, wrenching, grasping, scraping, clutching, covetous old sinner.*

For years after Marley's funeral the name still stood above the warehouse door. The firm was known as Scrooge and Marley. Sometimes people new to the business called Scrooge Scrooge, and sometimes Marley; he answered to both names: it was all the same to him. But Jacob Marley was as dead as a doornail. This must be understood, or nothing wonderful can come of the story I am going to relate.

ONCE UPON A TIME — on a cold, bleak Christmas Eve — old Scrooge sat busy in his counting-house. External heat and cold had little influence on Scrooge. No wind that blew was bitterer than he, and the cold within him froze his old features, nipped his pointed nose, shrivelled his cheek and spoke out in his grating voice. The door was open that he might keep his eye upon his clerk, who in a dismal little cell beyond was copying letters, and trying to warm himself at his candle.

"A Merry Christmas, Uncle!" cried a cheerful voice.

"Bah!" said Scrooge. "Humbug!"

"Christmas a humbug, Uncle?" said Scrooge's nephew, coming in. "You don't mean that, I am sure."

"I do," said Scrooge. "If I could work my will, every idiot who goes about with 'Merry Christmas' on his lips should be boiled with his own pudding."

"Uncle!" pleaded the nephew.

"Nephew!" returned the uncle sternly, "keep Christmas in your own way, and let me keep it in mine."

"Keep it!" repeated the nephew. "But you don't keep it."

"Let me leave it alone, then," said Scrooge.

"Don't be angry, Uncle," said his nephew. "Dine with us tomorrow."

"Goodbye," said Scrooge.

"I am sorry, with all my heart, to find you so resolute. We have never had any quarrel to which I have been a party. So A Merry Christmas, Uncle!"

"Goodbye," said Scrooge.

His nephew left the room without an angry word, stopping at the outer door to bestow the greetings of the season on the clerk, who, cold as he was, returned them warmly.

AT LENGTH the hour of shutting up the counting-house arrived. The clerk instantly snuffed out the candle and put on his hat.

"You'll want all day tomorrow, I suppose?" said Scrooge.

"If quite convenient, sir."

"It's not convenient," said Scrooge. "And it's not fair. If I was to stop half-a-crown for it, you'd think yourself ill-used, I'll be bound?"

The clerk smiled faintly.

"And yet," said Scrooge, "you don't think *me* ill-used, when I pay a day's wages for no work. But I suppose you must have the whole day. Be here all the earlier next morning."

The office was closed in a twinkling, and Scrooge walked out with a growl to take his melancholy dinner in his usual melancholy tavern; and having read all the newspapers he went home to bed.

NOW, there was nothing at all particular about the knocker on Scrooge's door, but Scrooge, having his key in the lock of the door, saw not a knocker but Marley's face. It was not angry, or ferocious, but had a dismal light about it, like a bad lobster in a dark cellar. As Scrooge looked fixedly at this phenomenon, it was a knocker again.

To say that he was not startled would be untrue, but he said

"Pooh, pooh," and closed the door with a bang. Once upstairs he put on his dressing-gown and slippers, and his nightcap, and sat down before the fire to take his gruel. As he did so, his glance happened to rest upon a bell, a disused bell, that hung in the room; and as he looked, the bell began to ring, and so did every bell in the house. Then came a clanking noise, as if some person were dragging a heavy chain. The cellar door flew open with a booming sound, and then he heard the noise much louder, on the floors below; then coming up the stairs; then coming straight towards his door.

"It's humbug still!" said Scrooge. "I won't believe it."

His colour changed though, when, without a pause, it came on through the heavy door, and passed into the room before his eyes. Upon its coming in, the dying flame leaped up, as though it cried, "I know him! Marley's Ghost!" and fell again.

The same face: the very same. Jacob Marley in his pigtail, usual waistcoat, tights and boots; the tassels on the latter bristling. The chain he drew was clasped about his middle. It was made of cash boxes, keys, padlocks, ledgers, deeds and heavy purses wrought in steel.

Scrooge fell upon his knees, and clasped his hands before his face.

"Mercy!" he said. "Dreadful apparition, why do you trouble me?"

"It is required of every man," the Ghost returned, "that the spirit within him should walk abroad among his fellow men, and if that spirit goes not forth in life, it is condemned to do so after death."

"You are fettered," said Scrooge, trembling. "Tell me why."

"I wear the chain I forged in life," replied the Ghost. "Would you know the weight and length of the strong coil you bear yourself? It is a ponderous chain!"

Scrooge glanced about him, but could see nothing.

"Jacob," he said, imploringly, "speak comfort to me, Jacob."

"I am here tonight to warn you, that you have yet a chance and hope of escaping my fate," said the Ghost, rattling its chains. "You will be haunted by three spirits."

"I — I think I'd rather not," said Scrooge.

"Without their visits," said the Ghost, "you cannot hope to shun the path I tread. Expect the first tomorrow, when the bell tolls one. The second on the next night at the same hour, and the third upon the next night when the last stroke of twelve has ceased to vibrate. Now look to see me no more, and remember what has passed between us!"

Scrooge followed him to the window. The air was filled with phantoms, wandering hither and thither in restless haste, and moaning as they went. Every one of them wore chains like Marley's Ghost; none were free.

Scrooge closed the window. He tried to say "Humbug," but stopped at the first syllable. And being, from the emotion he had undergone, or the fatigues of the day, or the lateness

of the hour, much in need of repose, he went straight to bed, without undressing, and fell asleep upon the instant.

SCROOGE AWOKE when the chimes of a neighbouring church struck the four quarters, so he listened for the hour.

The bell sounded with a deep, dull, melancholy ONE. Light flashed up in the room, the curtains of the bed were drawn aside; and Scrooge found himself face to face with an unearthly visitor. It was a strange figure — like a child; yet not so like a child as like an old man. Its hair was white as if with age; and yet the face had not a wrinkle in it. The strangest thing about it was, that from the crown of its head there sprung a bright clear jet of light, by which all was visible; and which was doubtless the occasion of it using, in its duller moments, a great extinguisher for a cap, which it now held under its arm.

"Who, and what, are you?" Scrooge demanded.

"I am the Ghost of Christmas Past."

"Long past?" enquired Scrooge.

"No. Your past." It put out its hand as it spoke, and clasped him gently by the arm. "Rise! and walk with me!" The grasp was not to be resisted.

They passed through the wall, and stood upon an open country road, with fields on either hand. The city had entirely vanished. The darkness had vanished with it, for it was a cold winter day, with snow upon the ground.

"Good heaven," said Scrooge, "I was a boy here!"

"You recollect the way?" enquired the Spirit.

"Remember it!" cried Scrooge with fervour — "I could walk it blindfold."

THEY WALKED along the road until a little market town appeared in the distance. Some shaggy ponies were seen trotting towards them with boys on their backs, who called to other boys in gigs and carts. All were in great spirits, and shouted to each other, until the broad fields were full of merry music.

"These are but shadows of the things that have been," said

the Ghost. "They have no consciousness of us."

They left the high road, and soon approached a door at the back of a mansion of dull red brick. The door opened, and disclosed a long bare school room, made barer still by lines of plain forms and desks. At one of these a lonely boy was reading near a feeble fire; and Scrooge sat down and wept to see his poor forgotten self as he had used to be.

The Ghost smiled thoughtfully, and waved its hand. "Let us see another Christmas!"

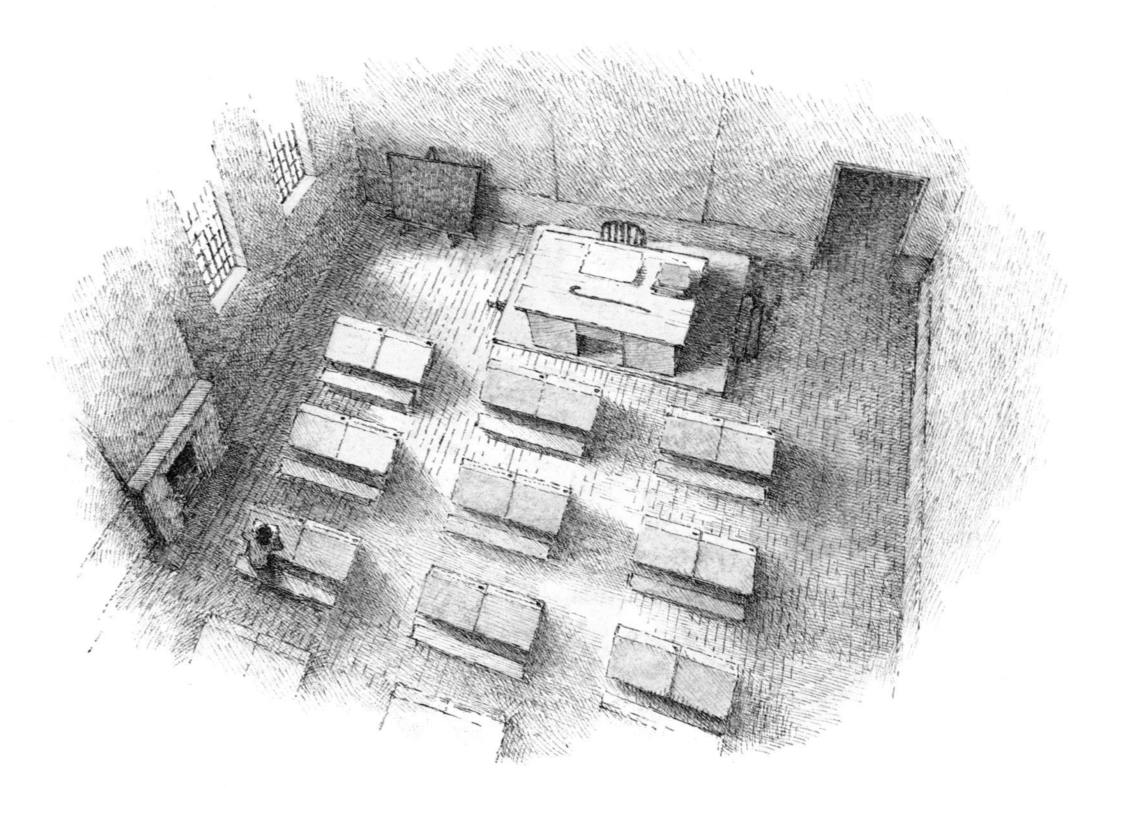

THEY WERE NOW in the busy thoroughfares of a city. The Ghost stopped at a warehouse door, and they went in.

"Why!" Scrooge cried in great excitement. "I was apprenticed here! It's old Fezziwig's!"

Scrooge's former self, now a young man, came briskly in, accompanied by his fellow 'prentice.

"Yo-ho, my boys," said Fezziwig. "No more work tonight. Christmas Eve! Clear away, my lads, and let's have lots of room here!"

Clear away! There was nothing they wouldn't have cleared away, with old Fezziwig looking on. It was done in a minute.

In came a fiddler, and in came Mrs Fezziwig, one vast substantial smile. In came the three Miss Fezziwigs, beaming and lovable. In came all the young men and women employed in the business, one after another. Away they all went, twenty couples at once. There were dances, and there were forfeits, and there were more dances, and there was cake, and mince pies, and plenty of beer.

When the clock struck eleven, this domestic ball broke up. Mr and Mrs Fezziwig took their stations, one on either side the door, and shaking hands with every person individually as he or she went out, wished him or her a Merry Christmas.

"A small matter," said the Ghost, "to make these silly folk so full of gratitude."

"Small!" echoed Scrooge.

The Spirit signed to him to listen to the two apprentices, who were pouring out their hearts in praise of Fezziwig; and then said, "Why! He has but spent a few pounds. Is that so much that he deserves this praise?"

"It isn't that," said Scrooge. "The happiness Fezziwig gives is quite as great as if it cost a fortune." He felt the Spirit's glance, and stopped.

"What is the matter?" asked the Ghost.

"Nothing," said Scrooge. "I should like to be able to say a word or two to my clerk just now. That's all."

"My time grows short," observed the Spirit. "Quick!"

Again Scrooge saw himself. He was older now; his face had begun to wear the signs of care and avarice. There was an eager, greedy, restless motion in the eye, which showed the passion that had taken root. He was not alone, but sat by the side of a fair young girl in whose eyes there were tears.

"You are changed," she said. "Our engagement is an old one. It was made when we were both poor and content to be so, until we could improve our worldly fortune by our patient industry. But you are changed. When it was made, you were another man."

"I was a boy," he said impatiently.

"If you were free today, can I believe that you would again choose a dowerless girl — you, who weigh everything by gain? For the love of him you once were, I release you. May you be happy in the life you have chosen!"

She left him, and they parted.

"No more!" cried Scrooge. "No more. Show me no more!"

"I told you these were shadows of the things that have been," said the Ghost. "That they are what they are, do not blame me."

"Remove me!" Scrooge exclaimed. "I cannot bear it!" He turned upon the Ghost, and wrestled with it. In the struggle Scrooge seized the Ghost's extinguisher-cap, and pressed it down upon its head with all his force, but he could not hide the light which streamed from under it.

He was conscious of being exhausted, and overcome by an irresistible drowsiness; and, further, of being in his own bedroom. He had barely time to reel to bed before he sank into a heavy sleep.

AWAKING in the middle of a prodigiously tough snore, Scrooge sat up in bed to get his thoughts together. Being prepared for almost anything, he was not by any means prepared for nothing; and when the bell struck one and no shape appeared, he was taken with a violent fit of trembling. He lay upon his bed, the very centre of a blaze of ruddy light. At last he began to think that the source of

this ghostly light might be in the adjoining room, and he got up and shuffled to the door.

"Come in!" exclaimed the Ghost, a jolly giant, glorious to see. "I am the Ghost of Christmas Present. Look upon me!"

"Spirit," said Scrooge submissively, "conduct me where you will. Last night I learnt a lesson which is working now."

Perhaps it was the kind, generous hearty nature of the Spirit, and his sympathy with all poor men, that led him straight to the house of Scrooge's clerk.

Mrs Cratchit, dressed out but poorly in a twice-turned gown, but brave in ribbons, which are cheap, was laying the cloth, assisted by Belinda Cratchit, while Master Peter Cratchit plunged a fork into a saucepan of potatoes.

"What has ever got your precious father then?" said Mrs Cratchit. "And your brother, Tiny Tim! And Martha warn't as late last Christmas Day by half-an-hour!"

"Here's Martha, Mother!" cried two smaller Cratchits, tearing in. "Hurrah! There's *such* a goose, Martha!"

"Why, my dear, how late you are!" said Mrs Cratchit, kissing her a dozen times.

"We'd a deal of work to finish up last night," replied the girl, "and had to clear away this morning, Mother."

"Well! Never mind so long as you are come," said Mrs Cratchit. "Sit ye down before the fire, my dear."

"There's Father coming home from church!" cried the two young Cratchits, who were everywhere at once.

In came Bob; his threadbare clothes darned up and brushed to look seasonable; and Tiny Tim upon his shoulder. Alas for Tiny Tim, he bore a little crutch, and had his limbs supported by an iron frame.

"And how did little Tim behave?" asked Mrs Cratchit as the two young Cratchits bore Tiny Tim off to hear the pudding singing in the copper.

"As good as gold," said Bob. "He told me, coming home, that he hoped the people saw him in church, because it might be pleasant to them to remember upon Christmas Day who made lame beggars walk and blind men see."

Bob's voice was tremulous when he told them this, and trembled more when he said that Tiny Tim was growing strong and hearty.

Back came Tiny Tim before another word was spoken, and Master Peter and the two ubiquitous young Cratchits went to fetch the goose, with which they soon returned.

Such a bustle ensued that you might have thought a goose the rarest of birds; and in truth it was something very like it in that house. At last the dishes were set on, and grace was said. It was succeeded by a breathless pause, as Mrs Cratchit, looking slowly all along the carving knife, prepared to plunge it in the breast; but when she did, and the long-expected gush of stuffing issued forth, one murmur of delight arose all round, and even Tiny Tim feebly cried Hurrah!

There never was such a goose. Bob said he didn't believe

there ever was such a goose cooked. Eked out by the apple-sauce and mashed potatoes, it was a sufficient dinner for the whole family; indeed, as Mrs Cratchit said (surveying one small atom of a bone upon the dish), they hadn't ate it all yet!

At last the dinner was all done, the cloth was cleared, and the fire made up. A certain compound in a jug being tasted, and considered perfect, apples and oranges were put upon the table, and a shovel-full of chestnuts on the fire. Then all the Cratchit family drew round the hearth, and Bob proposed:

"A Merry Christmas to us all, my dears! God bless us!"

"God bless us every one!" said Tiny Tim, the last of all.

He sat very close to his father's side, upon his little stool. Bob held his withered little hand in his, as if he loved the child, and dreaded that he might be taken from him.

"Spirit," said Scrooge, with an interest he had never felt before, "tell me if Tiny Tim will live."

"I see a vacant seat," replied the Ghost, "and a crutch without an owner, carefully preserved. If these shadows remain unaltered by the future, the child will die."

"Mr Scrooge!" said Bob; "I'll give you Mr Scrooge!"

"I'll drink his health for your sake and the day's," said Mrs Cratchit, "not for his. A Merry Christmas! – he'll be very merry, I have no doubt!"

The children drank the toast after her. It was the first of their proceedings which had no heartiness in it. Scrooge was the ogre of the family. The mention of his name cast a dark shadow, which was not dispelled for full five minutes.

After it had passed away, they were ten times merrier than before. They were not a handsome family; they were not well dressed; but they were happy, grateful, and contented with the time; and when they faded Scrooge had his eye upon them, and especially on Tiny Tim, until the last.

By this time it was getting dark, and as Scrooge and the Spirit went along the streets, the brightness of the roaring fires in all sorts of rooms was wonderful. Much they saw, and far they went, and many homes they visited, but always with a happy end. The Spirit stood beside sick beds and they were cheerful; in almshouse, hospital and jail, in every refuge where man had not made fast the door and barred the Spirit out he left his blessing and taught Scrooge his precepts. In a bright, gleaming room Scrooge recognized his own nephew, and found the Spirit standing by his side, and looking at that same nephew with approving affability.

"Ha, ha, ha! He said that Christmas was a humbug, as I live!" cried Scrooge's nephew. "He believed it, too!"

"More shame for him, Fred!" said Scrooge's niece, indignantly.

"He's a comical old fellow," said Scrooge's nephew, "and that's the truth; and not so pleasant as he might be. However, his offences carry their own punishment, and I have nothing to say against him. A Merry Christmas and a Happy New Year to the old man, whatever he is! To Uncle Scrooge!"

Uncle Scrooge had become so light of heart that he would have thanked him in an inaudible speech if the Ghost had given him time. But the whole scene passed off in the breath of the last word spoken by his nephew; and he and the Spirit were again upon their travels.

It was a long night, if it were only a night. It was strange, too, that while Scrooge remained unaltered in his outward form, the Ghost grew older, clearly older. Scrooge had observed this change, but never spoke of it, until looking at the Spirit he noticed that its hair was grey.

"My life upon this globe is very brief," said the Ghost. "It ends tonight at midnight."

"Tonight!" cried Scrooge.

"Hark! the time is drawing near!"

The bell struck twelve.

SCROOGE looked about him for the Ghost, and saw it not. As the last stroke ceased to vibrate, he remembered the prediction of Old Jacob Marley, and lifting up his eyes, beheld a solemn Phantom, draped and hooded, coming, like a mist along the ground, towards him.

"I am in the presence of the Ghost of Christmas Yet To Come?" said Scrooge.

The Spirit answered not, but pointed onward with its hand.

"You are about to show me the shadows of things that have

not happened, but will happen in the time before us," Scrooge pursued. "Is that not so, Spirit?"

It gave him no reply. The hand was pointed straight before them.

"Lead on!" said Scrooge. "Lead on!"

The Phantom moved away as it had come towards him. Scrooge followed in the shadow of its dress, which bore him up and carried him along.

They were in the heart of the city, and the Spirit stopped beside a little knot of businessmen. Scrooge advanced to listen to their talk.

"No," said a great fat man. "I don't know much about it. I only know he's dead."

"What has he done with his money?" asked a red-faced gentleman.

"I haven't heard," said a man with a large chin. "He hasn't left it to *me*. That's all I know."

This pleasantry was received with a general laugh.

Scrooge knew the men, and looked towards the Spirit for an explanation.

The Phantom glided on, its finger pointing. The scene had changed. A pale light fell straight upon a bed; and on it, beneath a ragged sheet, unwatched, unwept, uncared for, was the body of a man. He lay, in a dark empty house, with not a man, a woman, or a child to say "he was kind to me once, and for the memory of that I will be kind to him."

Scrooge recoiled in terror.

"Let me see some tenderness connected with a death," said Scrooge, "or this dark chamber, Spirit, will be for ever present to me."

The Ghost conducted him through several streets familiar to his feet; and as they went along Scrooge looked here and there to find himself, but nowhere was he to be seen. They entered poor Bob Cratchit's house; and found the mother and children seated round the fire.

Quiet. Very quiet. The noisy little Cratchits were as still as statues in one corner, and sat looking up at Peter, who had a book before him. The mother and her daughters were engaged in sewing. But surely they were very quiet!

The mother put her hand up to her face.

"The colour hurts my eyes," she said. "But I wouldn't show weak eyes to your father when he comes home, for the world. It must be near his time."

"Past it rather," Peter answered, shutting up his book. "But I think he's walked a little slower than he used these last few evenings, mother."

They were very quiet again. At last she said, "I have known him walk with — I have known him walk with Tiny Tim upon his shoulder, very fast indeed."

"And so have I," cried Peter. "Often."

"But he was very light to carry," she resumed, "and his father loved him so, that it was no trouble. No trouble. And there is your father at the door!"

She hurried out to meet him; and Bob came in. He was very cheerful with them, and spoke pleasantly to all the family. He looked at the work on the table, and praised it. They would be done long before Sunday, he said.

"Sunday! You went today then, Robert?" said his wife.

"Yes, my dear. I wish you could have gone. It would have done you good to see how green a place the graveyard is. I promised him that I would walk there on a Sunday. My little, little child!" cried Bob. "My little child."

He broke down all at once. He couldn't help it. He left the room, and went upstairs into the room above. There was a chair set close beside the child, and poor Bob sat down in it, and when he had thought a little and composed himself, he kissed the little face. He was reconciled to what had happened, and went down again quite happy. They drew about the fire, and talked; the girls and mother working still.

"SPECTRE," said Scrooge, "something informs me that our parting moment is at hand. I know it, but I know not how. Tell me what man that was whom we saw lying dead?"

The Ghost of Christmas Yet To Come conveyed him as before.

A churchyard. Here, then, the wretched man whose name he had now to learn, lay underneath the ground.

The Spirit stood among the graves, and pointed steadily down to one. Scrooge crept towards it, trembling as he went; and following the finger, read upon the stone his own name, EBENEZER SCROOGE.

"Am *I* that man who lay upon the bed?" he cried, upon his knees.

The finger pointed from the grave to him, and back again.

"Spirit!" he cried, clutching at its robe, "Hear me! I am not the man I was. Why show me this, if I am past all hope?"

For the first time the hand appeared to shake.

"Good Spirit, I will honour Christmas in my heart, and try to keep it all the year. I will live in the Past, Present and the Future. I will not shut out the lessons that they teach." Holding up his hands in a last prayer to have his fate reversed, he saw an alteration in the Phantom's hood and dress. It shrunk, collapsed, and dwindled down into a bedpost.

YES! and the bedpost was his own. The bed was his own, the room was his own. Best and happiest of all, the time

before him was his own, to make amends in!

"I don't know what to do!" cried Scrooge, laughing and crying in the same breath. "I am as light as a feather, I am as happy as an angel. A Merry Christmas to everybody! A Happy New Year to all the world! Hallo here! Whoop! Hallo!"

Running to the window, he opened it, and put out his head.

"What's today?" he cried to a boy in Sunday clothes.

"Eh?" returned the boy.

"What's today, my fine fellow?" said Scrooge.

"Today!" replied the boy. "Why, CHRISTMAS DAY!"

"It's Christmas Day!" said Scrooge to himself. "I haven't missed it. The Spirits have done it all in one night." He dressed himself "all in his best", and at last got out into the streets. Walking with his hands behind him, Scrooge regarded everyone with a delighted smile. He looked so irresistibly pleasant, in a word, that three or four good-humoured fellows said, "Good morning, sir. A Merry Christmas to you!" And Scrooge said often afterwards, that of all the blithe sounds he had ever heard, those were the blithest in his ears. He went to church, and walked about the streets, and patted children on the head, and found that everything could yield him pleasure. In the afternoon, he turned his steps towards his nephew's house.

He passed the door a dozen times before he had the courage to go up and knock. But he made a dash, and did it.

"Why bless my soul!" cried his nephew, "Who's that?"

"It's I. Your Uncle Scrooge. I have come to dinner. Will you let me in, Fred?"

Let him in? It's a mercy he didn't shake his arm off. He was made to feel at home in five minutes. Nothing could be heartier. Wonderful party, wonderful games, wonderful unanimity, won-der-ful happiness!

But he was early at the office next morning. If he could only catch Bob Cratchit coming late! And he did it; yes he did! The clock struck nine. No Bob. A quarter past. No Bob. He was full eighteen minutes and a half behind his time.

His hat was off before he opened the door. He was on his stool in a jiffy; driving away with his pen as if he were trying to overtake nine o'clock.

"Hallo!" growled Scrooge, in his accustomed voice as near as he could feign it. "What do you mean by coming here at this time of day?"

"It's only once a year, sir," pleaded Bob.

"Now, I'll tell you what, my friend," said Scrooge, "I am not going to stand this sort of thing any longer. And therefore," he continued, leaping from his stool, "and therefore I am going to raise your salary!"

Bob trembled, and got a little nearer to the ruler.

"A Merry Christmas, Bob!" said Scrooge, with an earnestness that could not be mistaken, as he clapped him on the back. "A Merrier Christmas, Bob, my good fellow, than I have given you for many a year! I'll raise your salary, and endeavour to assist your struggling family, and we will discuss your affairs this very afternoon!"

SCROOGE WAS better than his word. He did it all, and infinitely more; and to Tiny Tim, who did *not* die, he was a second father. He became as good a friend, as good a master, and as good a man, as the good old city knew. Some people laughed to see the alteration in him, but he let them laugh. His own heart laughed: and that was quite enough for him.

And so, as Tiny Tim observed, God Bless Us, Every One!

Little Baa
Kim Lewis
GUESS HOW MUCH I LOVE YOU
Sam McBratney
Anita Jeram
MAX
BOB GRAHAM
OWL BABIES
We're Going on a Bear Hunt
Michael Rosen
Helen Oxenbury
Maisy's Bedtime
Lucy Cousins
GORILLA
ANTHONY BROWNE
Leon and Bob
Simon James
JILL MURPHY
The Large Family
Five Minutes' Peace
HUG
JEZ ALBOROUGH
WHERE'S WALLY
MARTIN HANDFORD